THE
BRASS
KEY

Also by Caleb Wygal

Lucas Caine Novels
Moment of Impact
A Murder in Concord
Blackbeard's Lost Treasure
The Search for the Fountain of Youth

Mytle Beach Mystery Novels
Death on the Boardwalk
Death Washes Ashore
Death on the Golden Mile

THE
BRASS KEY

A MYRTLE BEACH MYSTERY
SHORT STORY

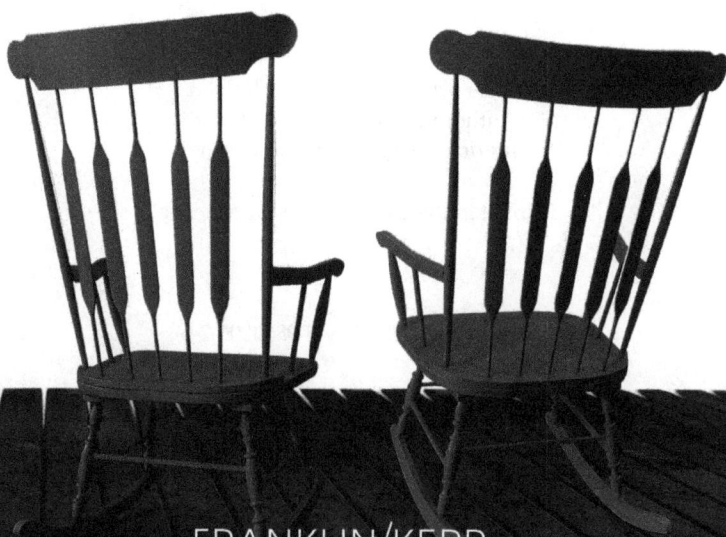

FRANKLIN/KERR
KANNAPOLIS, NORTH CAROLINA

CALEB WYGAL

Published by Franklin/Kerr Press
Kannapolis, North Carolina 28083
www.FranklinKerr.com

Edited by S. Daisy
Cover art and design by Mibl Art
Author photo by Pamela Hartle
Interior design by Jordon Greene

Printed in the United States of America

FIRST EDITION

Paperback ISBN 979-8-9860006-2-6

Fiction: Cozy Mystery
Fiction: Amateur Sleuth
Fiction: Southern Fiction

For JeRena

Thanks for the inspiration.

CHAPTER
ONE

"Look at these chubby women," Mark Whitman said to his wife, Peggy, of now fifty years. "Aren't they hilarious?"

Peggy looked over at her husband from where she was running her hands across a comfy sofa with a coral pattern near the front door and admiring the side table decorated with seashells next to it. His wide girth was hunched over, examining a collection of trinkets on a nearby shelf.

They found themselves in a neat store named Flamingo Porch in Murrells Inlet, about fifteen minutes south of Myrtle Beach, after the concierge at their OceanScapes Resort named some places where they might find some unique items for their home. The store had lofty ceilings and was packed to the brim with pre-loved furniture, decorations, jewelry, kitsch, and more.

Peggy tsked. "Mark, quit blocking the way."

He tore his eyes off the small statues of large women dressed in red and white polka dot bikinis wearing sunglasses in various poses, some provocative, and stood to allow a group of tourists to squeeze past.

"Sorry, dear," he said, his voice deep and gravelly. "But these are amusing."

"And have no room in our house," Peggy said. "You get these

little trinkets from everywhere and they sit and collect dust."

When Peggy and Mark went on vacation, they always came to Myrtle Beach, but rarely went to the beach. The largest tourist destination on the East Coast of the United States had so many things to do, and places to eat, that visitors often spent most of their time doing something other than having fun at the ocean. Peggy loved going to all the antique and consignment shops. Mark loved gorging himself on the many seafood buffets.

Their toes touched the sand once upon their arrival two days ago for a morning stroll on the beach. It lasted about one hundred yards before Mark got winded and had to turn back. Peggy could have walked for miles.

"Yes, dear," he said, stood, gave the figurines one last look with a smile, and squeezed his wide girth between the row of shelving and the side table next to the sofa Peggy stood before. "That's lovely."

"It is," she agreed. "It would look nice in our living room back home."

"It would. How would you do that? Tie it to the top of our Kia?"

She playfully slapped him on the arm at the image of hauling a long couch tied atop their red, boxy vehicle back to Reston, Virginia. She laughed. "We'd have to keep the windows down and hold on to it like people do mattresses tied to the tops of cars."

A rail thin woman wearing a white shirt and flowy skirt eased past behind them. She overheard their conversation. "I've seen people do that with golf carts around here."

The couple turned and regarded the woman like she was a bug. A silver name tag on her chest read "Sue."

"Golf carts?" Peggy said.

"Oh, yes. Those are the main mode of transportation for many people who live here," Sue said.

"You know," Mark said, "that makes sense. We passed several people driving down the frontage roads in Surfside Beach and Garden City on the way here."

"Not to mention the golf cart dealerships along the way," Peggy added.

"Oh yes," Sue said. "My husband and I have one as well. Anyway, we're having a twenty percent off sale today in photos and paintings." She waved a hand like Vanna White at the various artworks hanging above the picture windows at the front of the store and adorning the walls all the way to the back.

"Thanks," Peggy said. "I love the pictures of the sandpipers."

"Yes, they're lovely, aren't they? A retired schoolteacher who lives nearby paints them for us," Sue said.

"They are," Peggy said. Mark harrumphed. Art wasn't his thing.

Sue touched Peggy on the elbow. "Anyway, if you need anything, ask me or JeRena. She's at the back behind the counter. She owns the place."

"Got it. Thank you," Peggy said as Sue moved along to speak with other customers.

Mark and Peggy hadn't made it past the first ten feet inside the doors and had already been at Flamingo Porch for twenty minutes. Peggy saw the boredom in her husband's eyes already. "Hun, why don't you have a seat on this couch while I look around?"

He regarded the colorful sofa. "It looks comfortable. I think I'll do that."

With that, he plopped down on the cushions and spread a thick arm across the back of the seat. Sue drifted away as he settled in.

He'll be asleep within a few minutes, Peggy thought as she ran her fingers over the smooth surface of a polished dining room table.

Their three kids sent them to Myrtle Beach to celebrate their fiftieth wedding anniversary. Mark's health had been in a decline since he retired from his job reading water meters for the city a decade ago. He worked in the same position for thirty years while Peggy raised the children. They had a quiet, peaceful life, and rarely strayed far from home. She and Mark were high school sweethearts who married as soon as they graduated. Peggy went to a local community college to take art classes. Mark attended a trade school and mastered the art of welding. He became tired of it after a decade before getting a job with the utility company. She worked in a factory, hand-sewing shoe soles. They had three kids in five years, and after the last one started kindergarten, Peggy went back to work at the factory, this time as a shift supervisor.

The couple earned a comfortable living. She read books and painted landscapes in her spare time. He watched sports and hunted deer in the fall.

After he stopped working, he had a heart attack. Too much venison and beef. An ensuing open-heart surgery finished with complications. He almost died on the operating table and was never the same after that. The country boy fell out of love with hunting and sold his rifles but took up a greater interest in their grandchildren. They currently had five, and a sixth was half-baked. A brush with death made him realize time spent in the woods on the prowl for deer wasn't near as valuable as time spent with the grandkids. Besides, he wasn't a very good shot, and he'd be the first to admit it.

She meandered over to the front corner and saw a planter

basket with beautiful pink wisteria blooms and dangling ivy hanging from a window. They had little room for bringing back trinkets and gifts for the grandchildren, but the basket drew Peggy to it. She tried to reach for it but was too short. This was one reason she was drawn to Mark to begin with. He could reach the things on tall shelves.

"This would look lovely hanging on the front porch," she said to herself and looked back at Mark. His chin rested on his chest as he dozed. She called to him. "Mark!"

His head bobbed once, then his eyes opened. He blinked hard and searched for where he heard his name called from.

"Mark," Peggy said again. "Over here."

"Yes, Dear. Coming." He got to his feet and lumbered over. "What is it, hun?"

She pointed. "I want this basket."

Mark's head cocked from side to side. "It is nice. Front porch, you think?"

"I do. Will you get it down for me?"

"Of course," he said. Peggy moved aside so he could reach it. He plucked it off a hook. "There we go."

"Hold on to it for me. I'm going to continue looking around."

He smiled. "I'll resume my position."

Twenty minutes later, after a quick nap for him, and Peggy finding nothing else of interest that they could bring home, they left Flamingo Porch with the hanging basket in hand. After going through the same routine at a similar store nearby named Pluff Mud, they returned to their room on the 12th floor of the OceanScapes Resort in Myrtle Beach on the south end of the Boardwalk.

The room was typical. The view wasn't. Patterned beige

carpets underneath. The obligatory nautical painting above the comfortable king-sized bed. The small bathroom was nothing to call home about, either. However, two picture windows on either side of a sliding glass door leading to a spacious balcony provided panoramic ocean views. The sun was high in the sky to their right. A thousand points of light reflected off the tranquil Atlantic. A row of pelicans glided past their window as Mark let the hotel room door close behind him.

Peggy set the hanging plant down on the dining room table, adding it to the other trinkets they had picked up on their trip.

"That was fun," Mark said as he collapsed onto the bed. He stretched out one leg and propped the rest of his body up with the other foot flat on the floor. "My goodness, the traffic out there was insane."

"Nothing like back home," Peggy said, entering the kitchenette. "Are you hungry?"

"You know it," he said, patting his prodigious stomach. "What's in the freezer?"

Despite Myrtle Beach having one of the largest densities of restaurants per square mile in the United States, Mark and Peggy preferred to eat in most nights. She had placed a grocery delivery order after they checked in and received their room number to the local Wal-Mart. A delivery driver knocked on their door an hour later with several boxy bags filled with microwave dinners and soft drinks.

"Let me see," she said, opening the freezer door. "We got some Lean Cuisines and Smart Ones."

"Come on, hun. Don't hold back on my Hungry Man meals."

Peggy frowned as she watched her husband pick up the remote control and turn on the TV. The man always picked the worst things to stuff in his mouth, despite his doctor's warnings. She took walks every morning, ate well, and kept a trim figure. Mark played on the high school football team when she met him. He used to be a fit, but still husky, young man. Years of driving a city truck and eating fast-food lunches packed on the pounds. It reached a tipping point when Mark was in his early forties when his metabolism changed.

She plucked a blue box with yellow lettering from the freezer and closed the door. He didn't care which one he ate just if it put a dent in his hunger. Peggy knew from experience that the image of the delectable chicken dinner on the front of the package would fall far short of the finished meal inside. Expectations never exceeded reality with TV dinners.

Peggy popped the tray in the microwave before pulling a pre-made salad from the fridge for herself. She pulled out a chair and sat down at the table while his chicken nuked, moving the faux potted plant aside.

When she did, she noticed the corner of something poking out around the edge of where the soil met the plastic rim.

"Hmm," she said, pulling the plant back to her.

Mark had settled on watching a random college football game on TV. When she made the sound, he turned. "What's that, hun?"

"I don't know," she said, pulling the pot closer. "There's something tucked into the side of this thing."

"A hundred-dollar bill would be nice," Mark said with a laugh.

Peggy pursed her lips. She'd learned long ago to ignore her husband's wry humor. She grasped the corner of the thing sticking out. It was papery. "Hmm," she said as she withdrew it from the inside of the pot.

Mark lifted himself off the bed and trundled over. "What

the devil?"

In her hand, Peggy now held a small, aged manila envelope covered on one side by smudges of brown dirt. There was no dirt in the pot. Only the faux material used to simulate dirt. The mysterious object was no larger than a pack of Sweet'N Low and about as thick.

Peggy ran the object between two fingers. "There's something hard and thin in it."

Mark leaned forward to get a better look. "Looks like it's been there for years. Decades."

"Who knows?" Peggy said, not taking her eyes off the envelope in her hand.

"Well, what are you waiting for? Open it."

She turned the envelope over and examined both sides. There were no markings on the outside. A button held the flap shut. Peggy released it with a rattled *pop* and opened it. She looked inside. "Hmm."

"What is it?"

Instead of answering, she turned the package upside down and shook twice. A tarnished brass key fell into her open hand.

CHAPTER
TWO

"That's odd," Mark said.

Peggy agreed. "I'll say."

"What do you reckon that was doing there?"

"Beats me. Something someone wanted to keep hidden, maybe."

Mark leaned both elbows on the table to get a better look at the key Peggy held. The table shifted under his weight. "Looks like a tiny version of one of those old skeleton keys you'd see John Wayne locking up prisoners with in an old Western."

"It does."

The shine had worn off the key long ago. It was pitted and scratched in places. It was an inch and a half long and had a hollow barrel at the tip. The ring at the end reminded Mark of a bottle opener he had back home. Only smaller. The bit on the other end meant to fit into the lock had a grooved edge, meant to open its parent lock.

"I wonder what it goes to," Peggy said after a minute.

"Can I hold it?" Mark said, holding out a meaty hand.

"Sure."

Peggy gave the key one last good look with a furrowed brow before handing it to her husband.

He stood straight and rubbed the key between his fingers,

inspecting it from all sides. "There are no markings on it. No way to identify what it goes to."

"Reminds me of a key I had to a jewelry box my dad gave me when I was young."

Mark laughed. "So, this must be centuries old then."

Peggy slapped him on the arm but smiled. "Hey, you're no spring chicken either. I'll remind you that you're older than me."

"Pfft. Only by two weeks."

"Still, the fact remains."

"Yes, dear."

"Should we do something with it?"

Mark cast a skeptical eye. "Hey, we bought this fair and square."

"Yeah, but we don't own whatever this key goes to."

"True," he said, handing the key back to Peggy.

The microwave dinged with the completion of his Hungry Man dinner. Peggy started to rise, but Mark held her down by the shoulder.

"Stay put," he said. "I'll get it."

Peggy smiled at Mark's back as he made his way to the kitchen. He hadn't retrieved his own meal in years. She waited on him hand and foot, like her mother did with her dad. It was the way she was raised.

He opened the microwave door and set the tray on the counter, peeling back the plastic on top. Steam whooshed from the food. He took a fork out of a drawer and stirred the mashed potatoes. After grabbing a Dr. Pepper out of the fridge, he rejoined Peggy at the table.

"I wonder if that woman at the consignment shop would know where it came from?" Peggy said after Mark was seated.

"She might. We could go back tomorrow and ask."

"Sounds splendid."

Peggy stood, patted Mark on the shoulder as he stuffed a glob of food in his mouth and went into the kitchen to prepare her dinner.

Perhaps an adventure was just what the two of them needed.

* * *

The next morning, Mark and Peggy sipped coffee while sitting on the balcony overlooking the beach and ocean. The sun had completed its ascent into the sky. Light glimmered off the ocean. Thin cirrus clouds floated overhead. Waves broke onshore in a staccato rhythm. Seagulls squawked. Two small kids raced on the beach from their parents. Their squeals of joy reached Mark and Peggy's ears.

"That takes me back," Mark said.

"To when our kids were young?"

He nodded. "I wish we could go back to those times."

Peggy reached over and grasped Mark's hand. "Me too."

They sat and enjoyed their stale in-room coffee in silence for a few minutes before Mark said, "That's the thing with staying at these places during the off-season. The coffee sits there on the counters in those complementary baskets, growing old, and the coffee pots get blinky from disuse."

"Emily has it right," Peggy said. "They always take their own travel Keurig pot on trips with them. When they aren't flying, that is."

"She was always the pragmatic one. Unlike Richard."

"Well," Peggy said, raising her mug, "he always was the one who marched to the beat of his own drummer."

"That's the truth. Did you get them a Thank You card for sending us on this trip?"

"No, not yet."

"Maybe we'll ask the concierge if there's somewhere nearby where we can get one."

"Sounds good."

"I checked my phone last night," Mark said. "Flamingo Porch doesn't open until eleven."

"So, we have a few hours before that happens."

He drained the last of his coffee, stood, and gave the ocean one last look. "Beautiful. Let's get cleaned up and see what we can see."

Peggy was right behind him.

* * *

They piled into their older red Kia Soul. It was from the first year they made the vehicle. Peggy fell in love when she first saw the car commercials with dancing hamsters during a break in one of Mark's football games. The next day, she went out to the local car lot while Mark was at work and did a test drive. She loved the little boxy SUV and drove home in it after trading her aged and beaten Toyota Corolla.

That evening, when Mark got home from work and saw it in the driveway, he thought one of their kids was visiting, and figured that Peggy and whichever kid had gone out shopping. He knew Peggy would never leave him to fend with dinner for himself.

She had greeted him at the door with a beaming smile on her face and showed off her new ride. Then Mark tried to sit in the driver's seat. He didn't fit. His bulk spilled over the middle section and steering wheel.

"That's okay," Peggy had said. "It's mine to drive."

Mark could wedge himself into the passenger seat and crank the seat all the way back. Peggy was thankful that the kids were grown, and none would have to sit behind him.

On the rare times when she and Mark went out, they rode in his big, gas-guzzling truck. When it came time to go to Myrtle Beach, their first trip together in years, they agreed Peggy would drive so they could save money on gas.

Thus, on a sunny and warm morning in Myrtle Beach, they piled into the Kia. They had some time to spare before the consignment shop opened, so they drove around. First, up and down Ocean Boulevard, taking in the sights, the Boardwalk, the beach volleyball courts, the signature Sky Wheel and the high-rise hotels. Then they passed through a residential neighborhood on their way out to the 17 Bypass. From there they drove around Broadway at the Beach and saw another large Ferris wheel, the Pelicans minor-league baseball stadium, an upside-down house, a wax museum with King Kong hanging off a facsimile of the Empire State Building, and a scaled-down replica of the Roman Colosseum that housed a gladiator dinner show.

Mark had seen a leaflet in the lobby of OceanScapes, advertising the show, and mentioned to Peggy that he'd like to see it. She looked at the hunk on the cover who was the main character and decided it might not be a bad idea. She didn't catch his name, but she saw his face on billboards in the area too. The man must be famous around here.

As the clock approached eleven, they headed south toward Murrells Inlet and Flamingo Porch. When they pulled into the parking lot, only one car was there. A green Prius was nestled against the right side of the building.

They went inside. A bell dinged above the door upon entering. When they were here the previous day, Peggy hadn't paid attention to all the flamingos on display in the store. Now she knew where the place got its name. There were pictures of flamingos, shirts on a rack with the pink birds, decorations galore, and even one dangling on a rope from the ceiling.

The woman who sold them the pot stood behind the counter at the back of the store, going over a ledger with a yellow highlighter poised in one hand. She looked up at Peggy and Mark with distracted disinterest. "Good morning. Welcome. Any item you see with a red tag is twenty percent off today. Let me know if you need anything."

Peggy and Mark navigated through a maze of colorful sofas, chairs, accent tables, curios, and flamingos to reach the counter. JeRena, the owner of Flamingo Porch, looked up as they arrived. She recognized them.

"Oh, you were in here yesterday," she said, then smiled. "Come back for more?"

"Maybe," Mark said, taking the lead. "My wife here bought a hanging basket of fake flowers."

"Wisteria," Peggy added.

"Yes, I remember," JeRena said.

"Do you know anything about it?" Mark asked.

JeRena's eyes narrowed behind thick glasses with a bluish tint to the lenses. "Well, locals bring half of everything we carry. The other half are items we get from local estate sales. It seems like, if I recall, that the one you purchased came from a pair we bought at an estate sale a while back. They've been hanging there for a long time. I was almost ready to put it on clearance."

"Estate sale?" Mark said. "Like after people die?"

Peggy and JeRena made quick eye contact. Peggy rubbed a hand on Mark's arm. "Sometimes. Other times, they do those types of sales when someone moves and either needs to downsize or doesn't want to take everything with them."

"Yeah," JeRena agreed. "These ones, I believe, came after a local artist here in Murrells Inlet passed away. He had a big house out near the Marsh Walk."

"Oh, okay," Mark said, leaning against the counter, causing it to shift. "Remember anything about him?"

JeRena looked at the ceiling for a second. "Just that he was in his nineties and had been around here for a long, long time. He was quite prolific if memory serves. Single his entire life."

"Remember his name?" Peggy said.

"Hmm," JeRena said, tapping a finger on the counter. "Fitzsimmons or something like that. Sue might know. She's the artsy one here."

"Is she around?" Mark said.

JeRena shook her head. "Nope. She's off for a few days. I could ask her Saturday when she comes in if you're interested."

Mark held up a hand against the lip of the counter. "Nah, it's okay. No need to bother her."

"Actually," Peggy said, "that would be nice of you. I'll give you my number if that's okay?"

"Sure," JeRena said.

The bell on the door dinged and two blue-haired women who had to be sisters entered the store.

JeRena handed Peggy a Post-It note and a pen. After writing her contact information, Peggy handed both back to JeRena.

"I'll be sure to ask her," JeRena said.

"Thank you," Peggy said, then paused. "Wait, did you say that the pot we purchased yesterday came from a pair?"

"I did."

Peggy smiled.

CHAPTER
THREE

A few minutes later, Peggy and Mark were back in the Kia, this time with the other hanging pot of wisteria. It had been hanging in the opposite corner from where Peggy found the first pot the previous day.

She handed the pot to Mark while she put her seatbelt on in the driver's seat and cranked the AC. She said, "Man, it gets humid in this area."

Mark, whose forehead glistened with sweat from walking to their car through the parking lot, agreed. "You're telling me. I'm making my own gravy over here."

Peggy's stomach churned for a moment at that thought. She pointed at the hanging pot in his lap, atop of the stretched-out seatbelt. "Go ahead. See if there's anything in it."

Cars zoomed past on 17, headed for Huntington Beach State Park and Pawley's Island. Peggy turned the radio down low. Mark had found a classic rock station upon arriving in the Grand Strand. The notes of an old Allman Brothers Band tune played low on the stereo.

"Right," he said, adjusting the trucker hat on his head. He shifted the strands of fake wisteria around while the fingers of his other hand prodded between the dirt and side of the pot. A second later, he pulled out a small, smudged envelope and held it in the air. "Wow! I didn't expect to find anything."

The creme-colored envelope was square and curved after conforming to the curvature of its confined space for who knows how many years. There was no writing on it. He handed it to Peggy.

"Here, you do the honors," he said.

Peggy took it and noted its thinness. Whatever was inside wasn't thick or rigid like a greeting card, although this envelope might have come from someplace like a Hallmark. She placed a finger under the fold and slid it through. The paper *shhsked* as she did so. She lifted the flap and withdrew two sheets of folded paper. One was a hand-written note with elegant but masculine penmanship. The second was a boxy drawing of some sort.

For once in his life, Mark was quiet.

She opened the note and read aloud after clearing her throat. "To whomever holds this letter. I have kept a secret for far too long. I hope no one ever reads this, but here you are. When I was a youth, I had a secret romance with a girl whom I could never replace. I never found love again after her death. She was untouchable, but I found a way to touch her as she touched my heart. If you have both wisteria plants, then you also have a key. If not, search the other pot. You will find it in the same place you found this letter."

"Good thing we already have that," Mark said.

"That's the truth," Peggy said, then continued her reading. "The key goes to a jewelry box in her room. I know it is still there, even after all this time. Find it. Open it. Keep what is inside or share my story with the world. It is yours. Signed, C. Fitzsimmons."

"Wonder what it could be?" Mark said.

"Beats me. Something valuable. He never named the girl."

"I noticed that. What's that second sheet?"

Peggy slid the letter behind the second sheet. "It looks like the layout of a home. A big one at that." She held it up so Mark could get a better view. "See how many rooms there are?"

His lips formed a tight line. "Goodness. Must be a mansion of some sort. Maybe she was rich, and he was poor, and that's why he said she was untouchable."

"Could be. I wonder how we could learn more?"

"That Flamingo lady said her worker might know something, but she won't be here until the day after we're supposed to leave."

Cars began filling the lot as tourists and locals alike came to Flamingo Porch to see what was new and what was eclectic.

"Right. I hope she'll give our number to her worker before then."

A huge SUV pulled in next to them and eight middle-aged people exited the three rows of seats and headed for the front door of Flamingo Porch. "Looks like she's getting busy."

"This seems like a happening place," Mark said. "Want me to go back in and see if she can get our number to her friend sooner rather than later?"

"If you'd like," Peggy said. "I'll keep the car and air conditioner running."

"Good plan," Mark said, and opened his door. A wave of humid air rushed in as he climbed out. The shocks creaked as the car shifted back to level upon Mark's exit.

Peggy held the letters in her hand and watched her husband reenter the business. She couldn't recall the last time he showed the initiative to take the lead.

* * *

After Mark returned to the Kia, he said JeRena was doubtful the worker would respond.

"I doubt we'll hear from her before we have to go home," he said to Peggy.

"If that's the way it is, so be it," Peggy said, pulling out onto 17.

They hopped over to the Marsh Walk in Murrells Inlet and had lunch at the Hot Fish Club. The couple discussed the letter over lunch and what it could mean and tried to think of where to find more information. Peggy used her smartphone and entered a search string for "Fitzsimmons artist Murrells Inlet."

"His name was Claude," Peggy said.

"Claude? Don't hear that name often," Mark said while sipping from a pint of beer.

"He died recently. A year ago, it looks like. He was a prolific artist with paintings and sculptures. He was known for painting and sculpting the same woman in various poses and settings."

"Are there any pictures? Any of them naked?"

Her forehead wrinkled at the thought of her husband wanting to see nude pictures. "Let's see. Nope. They are all tastefully done. It is the same woman in every picture. I don't know much about art, but they are quite good."

Mark held out his hand. "Let me see."

Peggy handed him the phone and poked at her tuna salad. From their table, they had a view of the inlet. Kayakers paddled past on their way out to open water. Various sized boats motored past at idle speed. Their passengers were content to take in a beautiful day. A man with long hair strummed a guitar in a gazebo by the water. The melodies faintly made their way inside.

"They are nice," Mark said a minute later, handing Peggy back her phone. "The woman is always in a window, but in varied poses, doing different things."

She took it and placed it on the table. "I'll look at it more later. Right now, I just want to enjoy this lunch."

"Right. This red snapper is divine. Going to blow out the rest of our budget, though."

"It's okay. I brought an emergency credit card for special occasions like this."

"Does this qualify as a special occasion?" Mark said.

"Sure. We're on vacation and having a little adventure."

* * *

The OceanScapes Resort's check-in desk was across the street on Ocean Boulevard from the main tower with the pools and guest rooms. An open lobby with a high ceiling greeted them upon entry. Aerial photos from over twenty years old hung on the walls between windows, showing the construction of the resort in varying stages. Several "Best of Myrtle Beach" plaques dotted the wall behind the check-in desk.

A young man and woman were at the desk, pecking away at computers, when Mark and Peggy walked in. The man had dark, spiky hair, and a tan complexion. His name tag read "Ray." The other, Natasha, was tall, blonde, and curvy, with pale skin. He looked up to greet the older couple. She didn't.

"Good afternoon. What can I do for you?" Ray asked.

Mark walked up and leaned against the counter. Peggy stood beside him, fiddling with the strap of her pocketbook.

"Good afternoon to you, too," Mark said. "Got a question for you."

Ray smiled, revealing perfect teeth. Peggy thought that if

you're going to put your best face forward, this OceanScapes Resort was doing that by having these two at their front desk. Both looked like they belonged on the front of fashion magazines.

"Go ahead," Ray said. "I'm sure we can help."

"Just looking for some information," Mark said. "Do you know many people in the art scene around here?"

Ray tilted his head to the side. "Sorry, I don't. What about you Natasha?"

The shapely woman next to him had eavesdropped on their conversation. She had a heavy Slavic accent when she spoke. "I don't either."

Just then, a short, well-dressed woman with blonde hair walked up to the counter and interrupted. Her face was red, and she appeared out of breath. "Hey, you two. Make sure you put your timecards in after you clock out today. I need to get in here early in the morning and do the payroll so you can get paid this week."

"That's right," Ray said. "You're going on vacation starting tomorrow."

"Yep," the woman said. "My husband is packing the van as we speak. Headed to Daytona Beach."

"Sounds exciting, Paige."

"It does," Natasha said, without conviction.

Paige noticed Mark and Peggy standing there and held a hand to her chest. "I'm sorry. Did I disrupt your conversation?"

"You did," Mark said, "but it's okay."

"They were looking to see if we knew anyone involved in the art scene," Ray said. "Can you help?"

Paige tapped a finger on her chin. "I've been to a few events down at the Chapin Art Museum but can't say I know anyone involved. John Allen Howard recently moved up on the Golden Mile."

Peggy placed a hand on Paige's arm. "You mean the one who does the music for all those movies?"

Paige's chin dipped. "That's the one. The composer."

"Wow. Do you know him?" Peggy asked.

"No, but I thought that was a cool fact about the area, don't you think?"

"It is," Mark said. "Love that movie The Duelist. Didn't he win an award for doing the music in it?"

"I think so," Paige said.

"Have any of you heard of an artist from around here with the last name of Fitzsimmons?" Peggy said.

Paige looked at her two employees. They shook their heads. "Sorry, I haven't. I don't know that I can help you, but I have a friend who owns a bookstore two blocks up that might. His name is Clark. He's usually there drinking coffee. He knows a little about everything."

CHAPTER
FOUR

Peggy and Mark exited the lobby and stood on the sidewalk. Cars, trucks, mopeds, and golf carts crisscrossed on Ocean Boulevard in front of them. Two pelicans out for a jaunt flew by from right to left. The residential tower of the OceanScapes Resort loomed above them across the street. Travelers arrived in the parking lot hoping to do an early check-in.

Mark held a hand above his eyes and squinted up the sidewalk in the direction of the bookstore Paige mentioned. "I think I see it from here."

Peggy followed his gaze. Sure enough, two blocks up on the other side of a short second row hotel was a bright green strip of stores. It didn't look far for Peggy but doubted Mark's ability and stamina to make the journey.

"Do you have the letter and drawing?" he asked.

Peggy patted her pocketbook. "In here. Want me to get the car?"

"What for? It's right there. Come on."

He crooked out his arm and Peggy threaded her hand through it. She smiled to herself as Mark kept his face forward and chin held high. It had been years since she had seen him with this type of motivation or resolve to do anything besides run into their local Pizza Hut. She enjoyed watching mysteries on television while he watched sports in the other room. He never watched what she watched, but she would at least join him for big games. Maybe he liked mysteries more than he knew, especially now that he was involved in one.

Within a few minutes, they climbed two steps leading to a walkway that traveled the length of The Shops on the Boardwalk strip. The aroma of baking waffle cones greeted them. An ice cream parlor occupied the store space on the other end. Before that was a touristy t-shirt shop and a boutique for home décor. Maybe if, and after they talked to this Clark fellow, Peggy decided she and Mark could split up. A few things caught her eye in the windows of the home place while she figured he would be ready for a mid-afternoon sundae.

A rack of $1.00 books stood to the left of the door for Myrtle Beach Reads. The name of the bookstore was painted above the door. A hand-written chalkboard sign on the other side of the door read "The whole future lies in uncertainty; live immediately. —Seneca."

Mark laughed.

"What's so funny?" Peggy said.

He pointed at the sign. "That. I think we're following that advice for at least today."

She squeezed her husband's arm. "Maybe we should do things like this more often."

"I must say," he said, patting her hand, "I haven't felt this alive in years. I don't know if this will lead anywhere, but today has been fun."

"I agree."

Mark held open the door for Peggy to enter. A bell rung above the door, announcing their entry. A young couple scooted past them on their way out of the store. The man carried a fat bag of books. Peggy let go of Mark's arm.

Two racks of new release books greeted them as they entered. Peggy saw an Amor Towles hardcover she was in the middle of reading back in her room on the top of one rack. The newest John Grisham legal thriller was next to it. She picked it up and tucked it under her arm.

"Going to get that?" Mark said.

"I think so. I've had my eye on it."

"Here, let me have it. I'll carry it for you."

She handed the book to Mark. "Thanks."

The bookstore wasn't near as big as their local Barnes and Noble back in Virginia, but this place had a charm of its own. Nautical paintings dotted the white shiplap walls with a rustic finish. Jazz music played from hidden speakers at a low volume. Louis Armstrong's raspy voice sung about having all the time in the world. The corner of her lips curved upward. She could live here.

Mark ran his hand along the side of a bookcase and let out a low whistle. "These appear handmade."

A checkout counter on the right, a coffee counter on the left, and a seating area in the middle of the store broke up the front book displays. A group of wooden tables sat in the middle. No one was behind the coffee station. Where they could smell waffle cones before walking in, the bookstore held the aroma of fresh-brewed coffee. It tempted Peggy to order one.

There were three people in the store. One was an overweight teenager looking at a video game magazine. He kept having to brush his hair from his eyes so he could read. A petite woman with short blonde hair and designer eyeglasses stood behind the cash register, scribbling something on a clipboard.

Peggy's step faltered when she caught sight of the third person.

He was seated alone at one table facing the front of the store, sipping from a steaming, well-used Mickey Mouse mug. A glowing laptop sat on the table before him. He had stylish, light brown hair. Brown eyes with flecks of green around the edges gazed at the screen. A chiseled jaw line framed a two-day growth of facial hair. There was more salt than pepper at the edges of his chin.

"What is it dear?" Mark said.

Peggy touched a hand to her collarbone, eying the seated man. "Oh, nothing. But if Clark is here, that's probably him sitting at the table."

"My thought too."

Mark took the lead and wound through the store and tables. His girth pushed aside the empty chairs in the tight spaces between tables.

The man took a sip of coffee as Mark and Peggy approached. "Can I help you?"

His voice caused Peggy's ankles to quiver. She wouldn't tell this to Mark.

"Hi," Mark said, taking the lead again. "We're staying down the street at OceanScapes, and a woman down there said we oughtta speak to someone here named Clark."

"Let me guess," the man said. "Gloria or Paige?"

"I think her name was Paige," Peggy said.

"Blonde hair? Short?" the man said, holding a level hand up to his seated head level.

Mark pointed a finger. "That's the one."

"Why would she send you to see me?" the man said.

"So, you are Clark?" Mark said.

Clark raised his hands with a lopsided grin on his face. "Guilty as charged. What can I do for you? I mostly know coffee and books." He waved a hand around at the interior of the bookstore. "As you can see."

"Sometimes what you can't see is just as important as what you can," Peggy said.

"Smart," Clark said. "You must like mysteries."

Peggy tilted her head forward. "I do. I like the classics. Agatha Christie, Dorothy Sayers, and the like."

"Sounds like you and my mom would get along well," Clark said, then took another sip of coffee before setting the mug down on the table. He gestured at the empty seats on the other side of the table. "Please, have a seat. Coffee?"

It was a little late in the afternoon for Peggy to have a cup, but she would not turn it down if offered. As she pulled out a chair, she said, "I'll have one, yes."

"Me too," Mark said, collapsing into the other seat.

"How do you take it?" Clark asked.

"Black as night," Mark said.

"Just a touch of half and half with a touch of sugar for me," Peggy added.

"Coming right up," Clark said, then went behind the coffee counter.

Peggy and Mark watched as he poured two cups of coffee from separate carafes. After preparing Peggy's cup as she requested, he rejoined them, setting down two steaming mugs before them.

"Thanks," they said at the same time.

"Don't worry about it," Clark said, retaking his seat. "I took Mark for a dark roast kind of guy, so that's a Riptide blend from

Grand Strand Coffee. Peggy, that's a blend of light, medium blend of Columbian and Brazilian beans by Benjamin's Bakery. Figured you enjoyed a lighter touch with a little robustness. Both are local to the Grand Strand."

"And you got that from meeting us two seconds ago?" Mark said in disbelief.

"I did," Clark said. "Try them."

Peggy sipped hers before Mark. She noted that the color of it was just as she liked it as she raised the mug to her lips.

"Mm," Mark mumbled. "Perfect."

"Same," Peggy said, and hefted her mug. "This is perfect. Thanks. What will we owe for these?"

Clark waved a hand. "Nothing."

"Nothing?" Mark asked, the disbelief clear in his voice for the second time in as many questions.

"I have a personal rule," Clark said. "If I invite someone to sit with me at one of these tables and they get coffee or tea, it's no charge. We're just friends enjoying coffee and conversation. As it should be."

Peggy stared at the man across the table. His eyes darted around in tiny movements, taking in everything. She estimated him to be around the age of their kids. The touch of gray in his hair and on his chin, along with a few lines around his eyes, gave him a wizened air, but not one of pretentiousness. Like he had been through some bad things in his life. What it was, she couldn't know. He had the demeanor of someone who dealt with something catastrophic but must move on and live their life.

The invitation for her and Mark, total strangers to him, to join him at his table displayed a natural curiosity on his part.

"So, tell me," Clark said, "What brings you to Myrtle

Beach Reads?"

Peggy told Clark the story of going to Flamingo Porch, buying the hanging baskets, and what they found inside of both.

"Claude Fitzsimmons, you say?" Clark said after draining the last of his coffee. "I never met him, but I knew of him. You can find his artwork in homes all up and down the Grand Strand. He used to go to these juried art shows around here and win most of the time. They said he was a one-trick pony, only using the one woman in all his artwork. They always showed her inside a window. If you're going to do one thing, at least be great at it. And Claude was."

"Any clue who the woman in his paintings was?" Peggy said.

Clark let out a breath, looking at the ceiling. "There were always rumors among the locals. The ones who've been here for generations. This is going to sound like I'm going off track, but bear with me while I gather my thoughts. Been a while since I've had to think about any of this."

"We have all afternoon, sir," Mark said.

Clark wagged a finger. "No, no. Call me Clark. 'Sir' is my dad."

Peggy laughed. Mark snorted.

"Anyway," Clark said, "once upon a time."

"That's how all good stories begin," Mark said.

"Something like that," Clark said, not minding the interruption. "Unless the second half of that is 'then the murders began'"

Peggy cackled. Mark burst out laughing.

"No, that does not sound like a story I'd want to read," Peggy said.

"I might," Mark put in.

Mark hadn't cracked open a book since high school, but she would not call him out on it now.

Clark continued. "So, once upon a time, the areas south of here in Georgetown County were home to some of the largest producers of rice in the world. Enormous rice plantations. Wealthy families. The owners of these places were also among the richest at that time. We're talking early 17 and 1800s. By the early 1900s, most of those rice plantations died out and gave way to an influx of people. Those rich families that remained and passed down their wealth generationally. These people lived on a different level than you or I."

"Rice?" Peggy said. "That's interesting. Never knew that about this area."

Clark arched a brow. "I didn't either until I moved from Southern Ohio and started college here two decades ago. Anyway, this is where we circle back to Claude Fitzsimmons. He was a relative commoner. Back in the 1930s or 40s, I'm not sure which one, Claude caught the eye of one of these rich families' young daughters. Her family didn't want her to see him, which was understandable at the time in which they lived. They probably wanted her to wed into money. Claude Fitzsimmons would not grant them that luxury. In the end, it didn't matter. The girl caught polio, became paralyzed, and died at a young age."

Peggy put a hand to her mouth. "That's so sad."

"It was," Clark agreed. "The belief is that her death broke Claude's heart to where he never wed, nor had any interest in getting married. The woman in all his artwork was his vision of her as a grownup."

"How romantic," Peggy said.

"It is," Clark agreed. "Sad, but romantic."

"What was this girl's name?" Mark said.

Clark cupped his chin. "Hmm. Elizabeth Groom, I think. Not

sure what happened to the family after her passing. Their old plantation home is still open for tours. I think it's on the national register for historic places."

"Really?" Peggy said.

"I believe so," Clark said.

Although having never met the man across the table from her, he displayed an earnestness and honesty that made Peggy feel secure that she could trust him. She nodded once, as though she was reassuring herself. Then she fumbled with the zipper on her pocketbook, opened it, and withdrew the letter from Claude Fitzsimmons, the brass key, and the accompanying map.

She held it out to Clark. "These were stuffed in the hanging baskets. I think he wrote the letter and drew the map."

Clark accepted the items and read the letter first before shifting to the map. He studied it for a moment, then picked up the key and scrutinized it from all angles. He looked up at Mark and Peggy. "I've been there once before. My wife, Autumn, dragged me there years ago." He paused and shut his eyes.

Peggy and Mark shared a look but said nothing. She thought perhaps the man was remembering a better time for him.

Clark looked at the map once more, then slid it and the letter across the table. He tapped the diagram. "That's the Groom house. I'm sure of it."

CHAPTER
FIVE

Peggy's spine tingled as she and Mark exited the bookstore. The key. The letter. Clark's description of Claude Fitzsimmons and the woman he could never touch or have. Peggy had lived over seventy years and couldn't recall feeling this alive. Even Mark had extra pep in his step. She hadn't seen that since his days of playing high school football.

As they walked back down the sidewalk to OceanScapes, traffic on Ocean Boulevard had picked up. It was close to four in the afternoon. A time when most resorts and hotels began check-ins. Weary travelers were arriving, getting to their rooms, and trying to figure out what they were going to eat for dinner.

Waves from a rising tide broke onshore across the street. Shadows from the tall buildings lengthened as the sun began its trip to the horizon.

Mark said nothing about the ice cream parlor down from Myrtle Beach Reads after they left. Perhaps he was still full from lunch, or the thrill of adventure kept him from thinking about food.

As a family on a golf cart passed by, Mark said, "Can you look up that Groom place and see when they close?"

"Sure," Peggy said, withdrawing her phone from the

pocketbook.

While she did so, Mark said, "That was some of the best coffee I've had in a long time."

"Agreed," Peggy responded, tapping on the phone screen. "All we ever drink is the store brand."

"We should up our game. I'd wake up to that type of coffee."

"We have some roasters around Reston we could try. I see them on the store shelves."

"We'll have a look the next time we go grocery shopping. Any luck?"

Peggy held the phone up higher so she could see better. "Yes, looks like they close for tours at six. The place is about thirty minutes away."

"Hmm. Let's get back to the car and go down there. Whaddya say?"

"Sounds like a plan. I just need to go back to the room and freshen up a bit. Get us some water to go."

"Sounds like a plan. Give me a chance to make a pit stop."

* * *

Fifteen minutes later, they turned off Ocean Boulevard onto Kings Highway, headed for Pawley's Island. After passing through Garden City and merging onto where Business 17 ends on its southern end, the businesses on both sides of the highway fell away, leaving row after row of towering loblolly pines.

Peggy drove with one hand on the wheel. In a surprising move, Mark had grabbed her right hand and held it in the space between seats. She had seen a revitalization in her husband since she pulled the small envelope from the side of the hanging basket of flowers. Fifty years of marriage, and living with the same person every day, had settled them into a familiarity and daily pattern. The romance left years ago. They loved each other. Of that Peggy had no doubt. Their lives were bound together, till death do they part.

That didn't mean a general malaise hadn't settled over their lives. She became used to waiting on him, hand and foot. Like her mother did to her father. It was the way she was raised. Mark would not turn down delivery service to his favorite recliner. She'd spoiled him over the years to where she didn't know how he would survive if something happened to her. She saw it with her friends as they grew older. In some marriages, it seemed, one spouse couldn't live without the other.

If something happened to Mark, Peggy knew she would be fine. There would be an emptiness, for sure, but she would go on. Mark was a different story. These past twenty-four hours offered glimpses into what he could do if he chose.

She squeezed his hand and glanced at the GPS on the dash. Bob Seger sang about going "against the wind" on the radio at low volume. "Says we're about ten minutes away."

"Great," Mark said, his head bobbed to the tune. "Love this song."

"Me too."

The Kia passed Brookgreen Gardens and Huntington Beach State Park before entering the Litchfield area in Pawley's Island. The pleasant female voice from the navigation warned Peggy to turn left in a quarter mile. She put on her blinker and got into the left lane, giving a wave to a friendly woman in a BMW who let them over.

She got into a turn lane and waited for what seemed like an

endless stream of cars to pass by before turning into the driveway of the Groom Plantation. A long gravel road wound between stately oaks with streamers of Spanish moss shifting in the soft breeze. Mark rolled down the window and let his hand feel the breeze. The smells of fresh cut grass and salt air entered the car.

"This is lovely," he said.

Peggy agreed. After crunching over the gravel for several hundred yards, the oaks parted, and the estate came into view. "Wow."

Mark leaned his head down to get a better view out the windshield. "Looks like someone fixed up a big old house."

"They probably did."

"Don't get me wrong. It's nice and all, but…"

"But you were expecting more," Peggy finished.

"I was."

The Groom home was a two-story Colonial with clapboard siding and red shutters on the windows. A covered wraparound porch ran along three sides. An older couple rocked back and forth on a porch swing, looking out onto Clubhouse Creek. Three chimneys poked out of the roof. One on either end, with one in the middle on the backside of the house. A group of small houses were in the distance.

A graveled parking lot sat on one side of the house. Two cars were parked close to the entrance. An old Chevy SUV was parked near the back corner. A short bus with a Loris Senior Living graphic painted on the side took up half the lot.

Four people came down the steps, separated, and headed for the two cars as Peggy pulled in beside a newer Buick. She nodded to a curly gray-haired woman with thick glasses attempting to open the passenger side door of the vehicle. Mark unbuckled his seatbelt while Peggy waited for the woman to close her door.

A moment later, they stood side-by-side at the bottom of the steps. They had a view of the foyer inside the front double doors. A cluster of people gathered inside.

"Must be the old people from the bus," Mark said.

Peggy elbowed him in the ribs. "Come on. They're not too much older than us."

"You're not too far off. Got the map and key?"

She patted her purse. "Right here. I was reading some information while you were in the bathroom in the room. They give tours that leave the foyer hourly. Guests are welcome to stay and walk the grounds afterwards."

"Judging by the lot, with the two cars leaving, there might only be one person working this time of day."

"What are you suggesting?"

Mark looked at his wife and gave a sideways smile. "Up for a little mischief?"

* * *

They joined the tour group and stood near the back as the guide began her tour. There were eight retirees in total in the group, not counting Mark and Peggy. Five women. Three men. One was the bus driver.

"Cal and Beulah Groom started the Plantation in 1682," began the guide. She was dressed in a plum vest and matching pants and wore a nametag that read "Thea." "There was a continuous rice operation here for nearly three hundred years after that. They did things besides farming on the plantation, which I will highlight later in the tour."

After doing a brief history of the house and operation, the

group departed the foyer and scaled a flight of stairs to the second level. Thea droned on about life in the 1860s and the Groom's. Peggy tapped her foot on the creaky floor. She wanted the guide to hurry and show them the bedrooms.

There were five bedrooms in all on this level and one bathroom to share. After showing the group the master bedroom, bathroom, and three other rooms, Thea stopped at the last room on the right before the hall disappeared to the left.

A yellow rope was tied across an open doorway. It was a small bedroom by today's standards. White walls ensconced a tiny bed with a wood frame against the far wall, flanked by rustic nightstands. A matching dresser stood against the far wall. A cloudy mirror stood atop it. An old brush and comb lay nearby. On top of the other end of the dresser was a small, wooden box. Motes of dust caught in the rays of the setting sun coming in from a picture window floated in the air.

In one corner was an unfinished painting on an easel. It depicted a young man sitting in the grass under an oak tree.

"This was the room where Elizabeth lived back in the 1930s. She was a budding artist who unfortunately succumbed to polio when she was seventeen years old. This room has remained largely untouched since her passing. We only enter to dust and clean. Moving on . . ."

Thea led the group to the end of the narrow passage and rounded a corner. Mark and Peggy followed the group until the two people in front of them turned right. Mark grasped Peggy's hand, holding her in place.

She looked up at him. He wiggled his eyebrows back toward Elizabeth's room. Peggy nodded and crept on tiptoes to the empty room. The floor creaked as she touched down at the doorway.

They stopped in place and looked down the hall in the direction of the tour group.

Peggy counted a silent five before releasing her breath. She didn't know what would happen if Thea caught them lagging.

They ducked under the yellow rope and into the room. This room had a mustier smell than the rest of the house. Peggy figured it was because the caretakers had changed little since Elizabeth's death.

Mark walked over to the window and looked out. He whispered, "Peggy, come here."

She joined him. He pointed at a tree outside and then at the picture. Peggy understood. The same tree from the painting in the corner. "Oh, I bet that's Claude."

"I think you're right," Mark said.

Peggy's heart broke. Elizabeth and Claude were each other's muse. She painted him. He painted her. For their entire lives. One short. One long.

Tears welled in her eyes. Mark wiped one out of the corner of his and sniffled. She wrapped an arm around him as they gazed at the painting. Elizabeth had painted the picture from the viewpoint of the window. It depicted Claude sitting in the grass with one leg splayed out with a shock of blonde hair. He wore an impish grin.

Peggy realized it was only a matter of time before the guide noticed their absence. She and Mark had to get moving. There wasn't much in the room. Her eyes went to the wooden box on the dresser.

"He must have snuck onto the estate to see her," Peggy said.

"Probably so."

She grabbed Mark's arm and pointed at it. She whispered,

"Over there."

They crossed the room together to stand in front of the dresser. The wood box was plain. No decoration. The only ornamentation was a lock binding the lid to the storage compartment.

Peggy unzipped her pocketbook and withdrew the aged bronze key. She held it up. "Here goes."

She placed one hand on the back of the box to hold it in place and stuck the key in the lock. Holding her breath, she turned the key. The lock clicked. The lid loosened.

She tilted the box toward them and raised the lid.

"Oh, my goodness," Mark said.

Tears streamed down Peggy's face.

Inside was an old black-and-white photograph. It showed a young Elizabeth and Claude, standing by the old oak outside, holding hands. Their smile said it all.

CHAPTER
SIX

Mark and Peggy rejoined the tour on the other end of the house. Thea didn't seem to notice them being gone.

They kept the photograph in the box but left the lid up. Peggy hoped someone would notice that the box that had been locked for nearly one hundred years was now open and would find and understand what was inside. If not, she and Mark had had their grand adventure.

After the tour ended, they lounged in a pair of rocking chairs holding hands in the narrow gap between, swaying with the salty breeze, and watching the sunset. The sky was a swirl of oranges, purples, and reds.

Mark laughed.

"What is it?" Peggy asked.

"That Clark guy said something to me on the way out of his bookstore."

"Yeah, what was that?"

"Sometimes, the adventure is the treasure."

And it was.

* * *

Two decades later, after both Mark and Peggy passed, their great granddaughter made a discovery as they emptied their house in Reston, Virginia. In the back corner, on the top shelf of a curio cabinet in the corner of their dusty living room, lay a single, unmarked brass key.

Read what happens the day after Mark and Peggy's adventure in *Death on the Boardwalk: Book 1* of the *Myrtle Beach Mysteries* by Caleb Wygal, starring bookstore owner, Clark Thomas.

All books in the series are available on Amazon, Barnes and Noble, Books-a-Million, and wherever books are sold. Don't see them in your local store or library? Ask the bookseller or librarian to order them for you.

Learn more on his website at calebwygal.com.

ABOUT THE
AUTHOR

Caleb is a member of the International Thriller Writers and Southeastern Writers Association, the author of five novels, social media marketer, woodworker, occasional golfer, reacher of things on high shelves, beach walker, shark tooth finder, and munchkin wrangler.

His two Lucas Caine Adventure novels, *Blackbeard's Lost Treasure* and *The Search for the Fountain of Youth*, were both Semi-Finalists for the Clive Cussler Adventure Awards Competition.

He is currently at work on the next book in the Myrtle Beach Mystery Series.

He lives in Myrtle Beach with his wife and son (the munchkin).

Visit Caleb online at
www.CalebWygal.com

*If you enjoyed this story please
consider reviewing it online and at Goodreads,
and recommending it to family and friends.*